Fairy Tale

by

____

Formatted by

Gimmicky Pseudonym

Dedication:

CHAPTER ONE

ACKNOWLEDGEMENTS

I'd like to thank Gimmicky Pseudonym for creating this book
to house my writing talent

OTHER BOOKS IN THE BLANK BOOK SERIES.

The Girl in the Title

Summer Beach

Silhouette of a Man

Not Lost in Space But Still in a Lot of Trouble

Journey to a Destination

My Life So Far

Fairy Tale